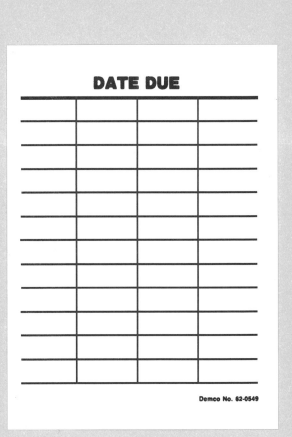

DATE DUE

Demco No. 62-0549

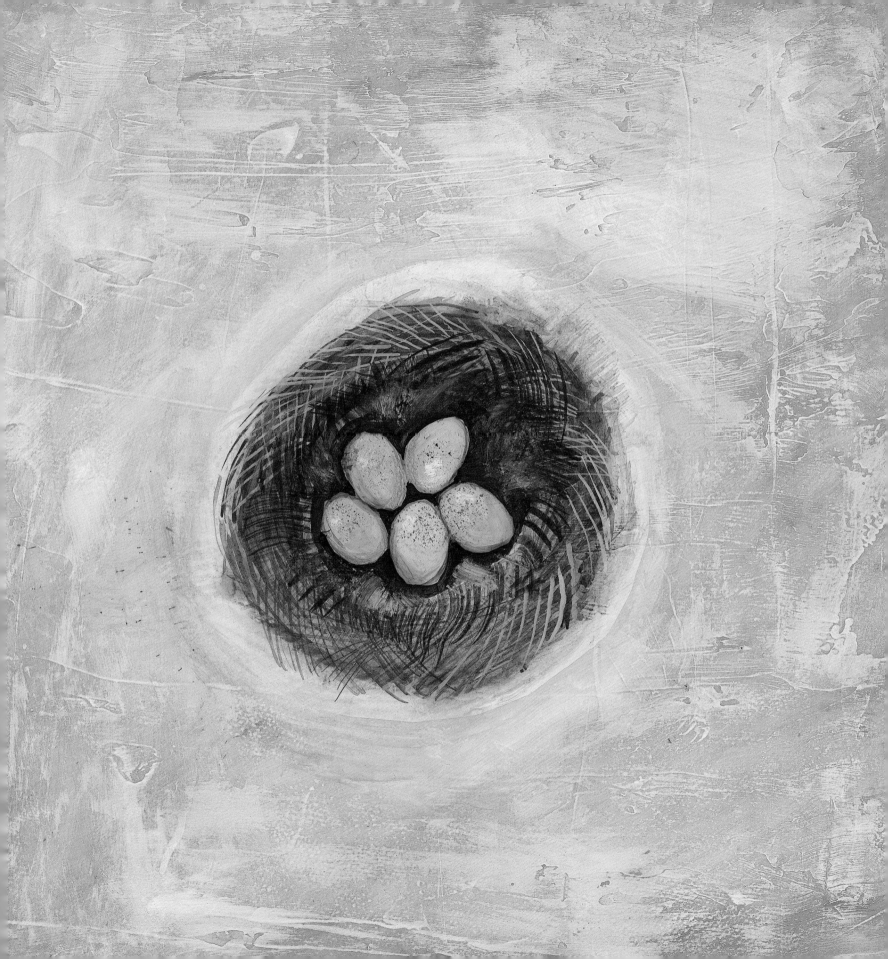

by DEBORAH HOPKINSON

Bluebird Summer

illustrated by

BETHANNE ANDERSEN

GREENWILLOW BOOKS An Imprint of HarperCollinsPublishers

Every summer my little brother, Cody, and I go to the farm on the ridge.

It's not much of a farm anymore. The wheat fields are still there, washing up against the barn like a golden sea, but they belong to someone else now. Since Grandma died, Gramps has sold them off, one by one.

Gramps says he never thought he'd miss the hot taste of dust in his mouth. Or getting up before dawn to plow. But Gramps misses lots of things now, Grandma most of all.

I miss Grandma, too. I miss watching her roll out piecrust smooth as an eggshell. And how she perched on a stool beside the tub and read us stories until our fingers pruned up. I even miss helping her weed the garden.

Grandma did not believe in neat rows. Her garden was a maze of marigolds, bluebells, sunflowers, and morning glories. You could wander through and munch sweet snow peas, hot yellow tomatoes, and crunchy baby carrots—if you didn't mind brushing off the dirt.

This summer, though, Grandma's garden is just a tangle of thistles and grass. Here and there a few flowers push through a curtain of weeds.

Something else is different, too. The bluebirds are gone.

Cody noticed it first. One night at supper he blurted, "Did the bluebirds leave because of Grandma?"

I kicked him under the table. We were under orders from Mom not to upset Gramps.

But Cody kept on. "Did they only come because they liked Grandma?"

Gramps scratched his head. "Why, no, Cody. Most likely they're not around anymore 'cause of those new houses across the way. The old trees the birds used to nest in got cut down."

I guess Cody got Gramps wondering, though. Because later when I went to say good night, I found him staring at the garden fence, as if he'd just noticed there hadn't been a bluebird on it for a long time.

That night I lay awake watching moonlight flick across the quilt Grandma had made for me when I was born. Gramps was probably right about the bluebirds, I thought.

Then I remembered something Grandma once told me. "I have a deal with the bluebirds, Mags. I grow some of their favorite plants—holly, honeysuckle, and Virginia creeper. And in return, they come sit on the fence each morning, warbling in the new day."

But how could the bluebirds find these plants now when the garden was smothered by weeds?

So next morning I pulled on my jeans and
grabbed Grandma's sun hat from the peg.
Gramps watched from the kitchen window,
swirling the coffee around in his old cracked mug.
"I ain't touched it in almost a year, Mags,"
he called out after a bit. "Too far gone now."
I pulled hard on a big thistle. "Just puttering."
"Humph. Like your grandmother."

ramps used to say that once Grandma started puttering in the garden, she was harder to get out than a dandelion. She'd be digging and weeding before we woke up, and again after supper, when the sun let go its hot grip.

Cody, Gramps, and I would sit slurping huge slices of watermelon, laughing to see who could spit seeds the farthest. Around us night would settle into stillness. Only Grandma moved, bending and rising like a tall heron at the edge of the water.

Gramps would call out, "Come on, hon, take a load off your feet."

Her voice would drift back, soft as a sighing pine. "Just puttering."

ext day we drove to town so Gramps could get some nails. We don't have anything like Mr. Nelson's store in the city. It has every size of shovel, rake, and hammer you can think of. Bins and bins of nails. Sacks of feed piled outside like hills.

"Where'd that curious Cody get to, Mags?" asked Gramps when it was time to go.

I finally found Cody sitting on a bag of black sunflower seeds, reading something.

"Let's go. Gramps is waiting."

"Look," he said, holding it up for me to see.

I shook my head. "Not now. Come on. Gramps will be mad."

But Gramps was chatting with Mr. Nelson about the price of wheat. He held out a cardboard carton full of little plants. "Here you go, Mags."

We came home with beans, zinnias and snapdragons, yellow marigolds and purple-faced pansies, cucumbers and tomatoes. We would putter after all.

worked in the garden every morning. Gramps had
chores to do, so he didn't have much time to help.
And Cody just got in the way.

First he tried to weed.

"Cody! Don't pull that—it's a flower."

Then he tried to dig.

"Cody, watch out!"

Then he tried to plant.

"Not like that, you'll tear the roots!"

Cody threw down his trowel. "You never let me help."

"All right, you can, but . . ." Too late. He was gone.

After that Cody took to wandering off by himself.

But sometimes I'd see him walking along the fence. I
wondered if he was doing what I was—watching for
a flash of blue that never came.

Our tomato plants grew fast. One morning Gramps helped me set cages around them.

After a while he straightened up. "Sun's too hot for me. I'll round up Cody and make lunch."

But when Gramps called for Cody, there was no answer. At first we weren't worried. But then a whole hour went by. I looked all over the orchard. I even poked my head down the old empty well, though Cody knew better than to go near there! I went through the pasture to the creek. I looked all over the house. I felt an awful fear coming up into my mouth, like I might get sick.

Gramps had just decided to call for help when the phone rang.

All the way to town, Gramps drove without talking, his hands gripping the steering wheel. Cody was right where Mr. Nelson had told him to stay put, on a sack outside the store. He didn't notice that Gramps was wound up tight as bindweed on a fence pole.

"Look what I got!" Cody called. "I bought it with my own money."

Gramps didn't even look. His voice sounded rough as new sandpaper. "What got into your head, Cody, to traipse two miles down here and worry us like that?"

"It's made especially for them," said Cody.

I shook his arm. "Cody!"

"We can put it along the pasture fence, Mags, near your garden," Cody persisted. "I bet they'll come back then."

Gramps stepped back. "Whatever are you talking about, son?"

"The bluebirds, Gramps. I've been reading all about them. It's hard for bluebirds now. They need special houses to keep their babies safe from other birds and animals." Cody held up a new wooden birdhouse. "I wanted to help, too," he said. "I want to bring back Grandma's bluebirds."

Gramps opened his mouth to say something, then stopped.

We stood still a moment.

It was one of those moments that gathers everything into it. It gathered the birdhouse and the garden. It gathered us and our love for Grandma and all our summer days and nights together. The moment was so full—it had so much in it—I felt like something just had to burst.

And it did.

All at once Gramps began to laugh. His laugh was soft at first. I thought he might be crying. But then he laughed so hard Cody and I just had to join in. We stood in front of Mr. Nelson's store and laughed together a long time.

I hope our laughter that day got carried on the wind like seeds, to a far-off place where bluebirds might hear it. And if they do, maybe it will remind them of an old farm, a garden, and a woman moving gently as a heron.

And so next spring maybe they will come back. They'll nest in the special bluebird boxes Cody and Gramps are building. They'll eat berries and insects from the garden. And they'll sit on the fence each morning, warbling in the new day.

I think Gramps will like that.

EASTERN BLUEBIRD

MOUNTAIN BLUEBIRD

WESTERN BLUEBIRD

ABOUT BLUEBIRDS

Have you ever seen a bluebird in the wild? You might be surprised to learn that bluebirds were once one of America's most common birds. But their numbers declined early last century partly due to the building of houses, malls, and highways, and the disappearance of old trees and wooden fence posts. Bluebirds are cavity nesters. That means they like to build their nests in holes in old trees and fences. The decline in the bluebird population was also caused in part by the introduction of house sparrows and European starlings, aggressive birds that compete with bluebirds for nesting sites.

Today bluebirds are making a recovery in some areas, thanks to the efforts of ordinary people who are building bluebird boxes and creating bluebird trails to encourage bluebird nesting. (A bluebird trail is a series of nest boxes placed where they can be monitored.)

There are three species of bluebirds in the United States: Eastern bluebirds, Mountain bluebirds, and Western bluebirds. Although this story was inspired by seeing Western bluebirds near my home in Washington State, Eastern bluebirds have faced the greatest danger. The bluebirds pictured in this book are Eastern bluebirds.

Bluebirds like to eat insects in summer and wild berries in winter. Their nests are shaped like cups and are usually made of woven grass. Bluebirds can lay up to six or seven light blue eggs, but three to four eggs is the more usual number. Bluebirds usually have two broods per season. They nest in the spring, in March to mid-April, but the exact time depends on location and weather.

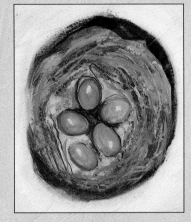

If you'd like to learn more about bluebirds or learn how to build a bluebird box, you can find information at your local library, at the many Web sites on the Internet, or by contacting the North American Bluebird Society (www.nabluebirdsociety.org or P.O. Box 74, Darlington, WI 53530-0074).

—Deborah Hopkinson

For Jeanne, Wayne, and Ara, who know about gardens, living
on ridges, and the importance of the price of wheat. —D.H.

For the experiences in life that have taught me that if you can be
patient through spring, the bluebirds return—always. —B.A.

Special thanks to The North American Bluebird Society, and to Myrna Pearman,
biologist, Ellis Bird Farm, Ltd., for her thoughtful reading of my manuscript
and her factual comments about bluebirds. —D.H.

Bluebird Summer
Text copyright © 2001 by Deborah Hopkinson.
Illustrations copyright © 2001 by Bethanne Andersen.
All rights reserved. Printed in Singapore by Tien Wah Press.
www.harperchildrens.com

Gouache and oil paints were used to prepare the full-color art. The text type is Palatino.

Library of Congress Cataloging-in-Publication Data

Hopkinson, Deborah.
Bluebird summer / by Deborah Hopkinson ; illustrated by Bethanne Andersen.
p.   cm.
"Greenwillow Books."
Summary: Gramps's farm isn't the same after Grandma's death, but slowly Mags and
Cody work to recreate her spirit by bringing back some of the things she loved.
ISBN 0-688-17398-5 (trade).   ISBN 0-688-17399-3 (lib. bdg.)   [1. Farm life—Fiction.
2. Grandparents—Fiction.] I. Andersen, Bethanne, (date) ill. II. Title.
PZ7.H778125 Bl 2001   [E]—dc21   00-032112

First Edition 10 9 8 7 6 5 4 3 2 1